GRAPHIC MYTHICAL CREATURES

GIANTS

BY GARY JEFFREY
ILLUSTRATED BY NICK SPENDER

Gareth Stevens
Publishing

Please visit our website, www.garethstevens.com.
For a free color catalog of all our high-quality books,
call toll free 1-800-542-2595 or fax 1-877-542-2596.

Library of Congress Cataloging-in-Publication Data

Jeffrey, Gary.
Giants / Gary Jeffrey.
p. cm. — (Graphic mythical creatures)
Includes index.
ISBN 978-1-4339-6035-2 (pbk.)
ISBN 978-1-4339-6036-9 (6-pack)
ISBN 978-1-4339-6034-5 (library binding)
1. Giants—Juvenile literature. I. Title.
GR560.J43 2011
398'.45—dc22
2010050922

First Edition

Published in 2012 by
Gareth Stevens Publishing
111 East 14th Street, Suite 349
New York, NY 10003

Copyright © 2012 David West Books

Designed by David West Books
Editor: Ronne Randall

Photo credits:
p5, Chmee2

Printed in China

CPSIA compliance information: Batch #DS11GS: For further information contact Gareth Stevens, New York, New York at 1-800-542-2595.

CONTENTS

Tall Stories

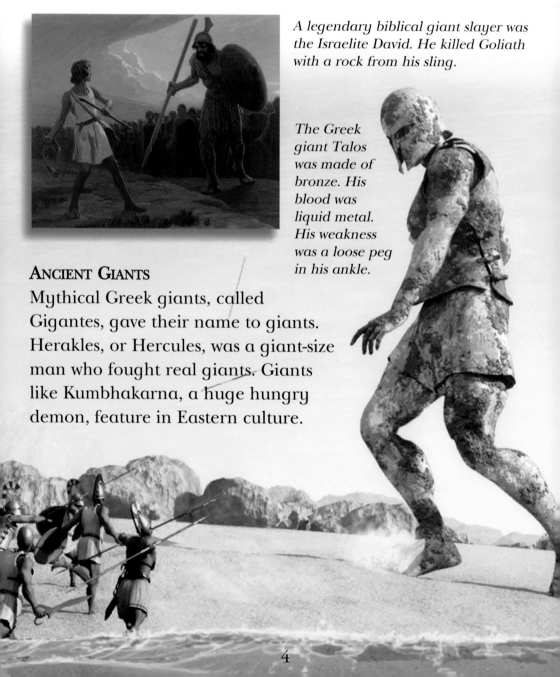

Mythical giants can be as tall as a house or the size of a mountain. Years ago, people believed that giants had walked the earth but were long gone. All that was left were huge bones, strange landmarks, and stories...

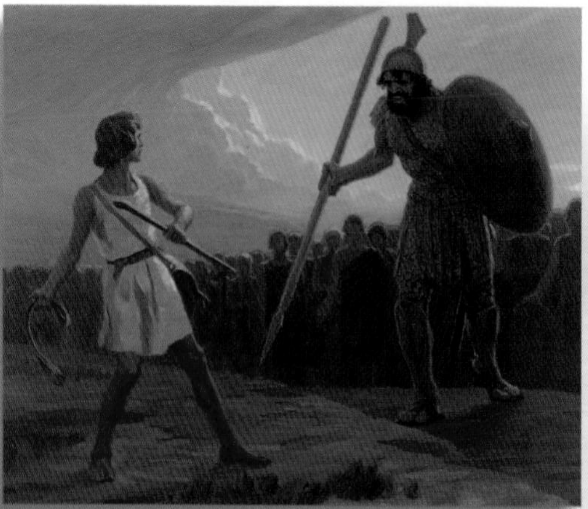

A legendary biblical giant slayer was the Israelite David. He killed Goliath with a rock from his sling.

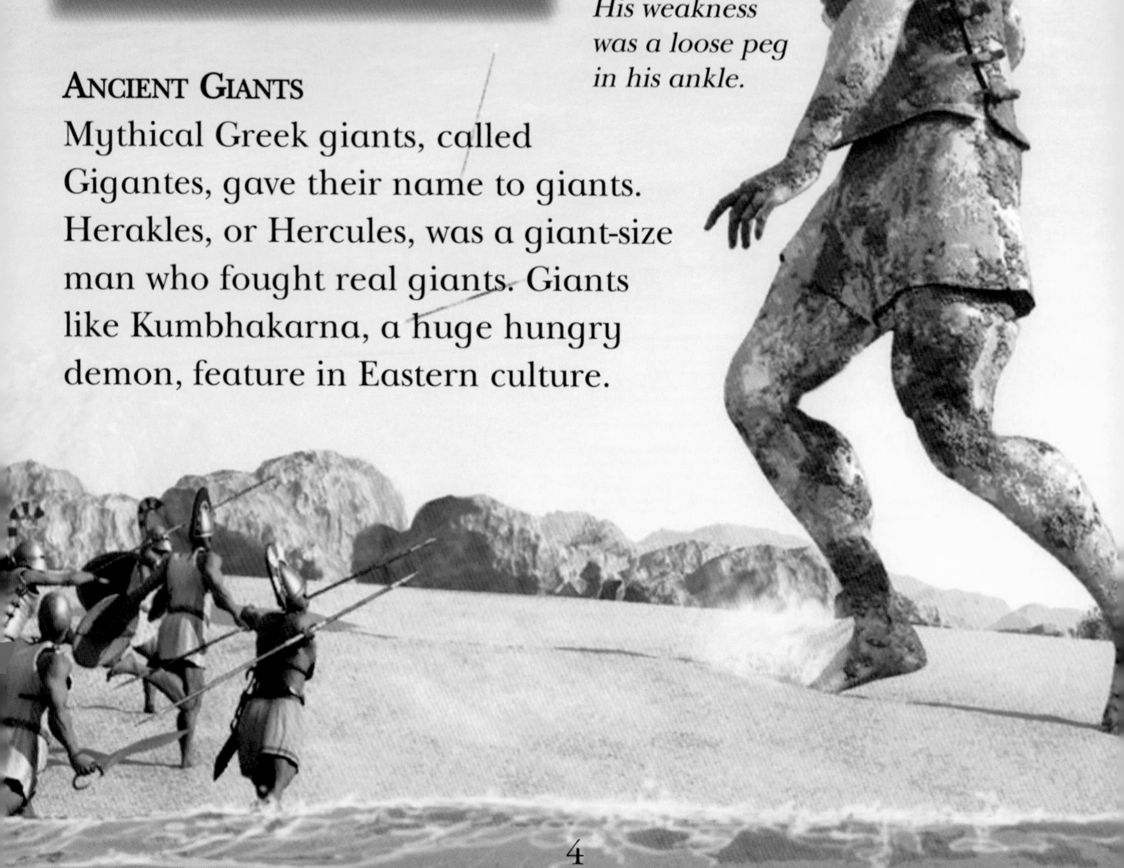

The Greek giant Talos was made of bronze. His blood was liquid metal. His weakness was a loose peg in his ankle.

Ancient Giants

Mythical Greek giants, called Gigantes, gave their name to giants. Herakles, or Hercules, was a giant-size man who fought real giants. Giants like Kumbhakarna, a huge hungry demon, feature in Eastern culture.

Giant Features

Unusual land features showed where mythical giants had been. Huge stones that stood in fields, ancient palaces with walls made of massive boulders, and vast, rock-paved roads were all once thought to be the handiwork of giants.

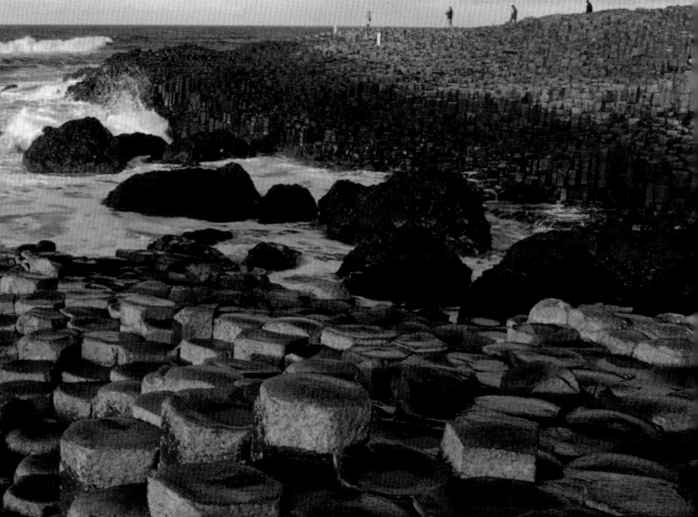

The Giant's Causeway in Northern Ireland

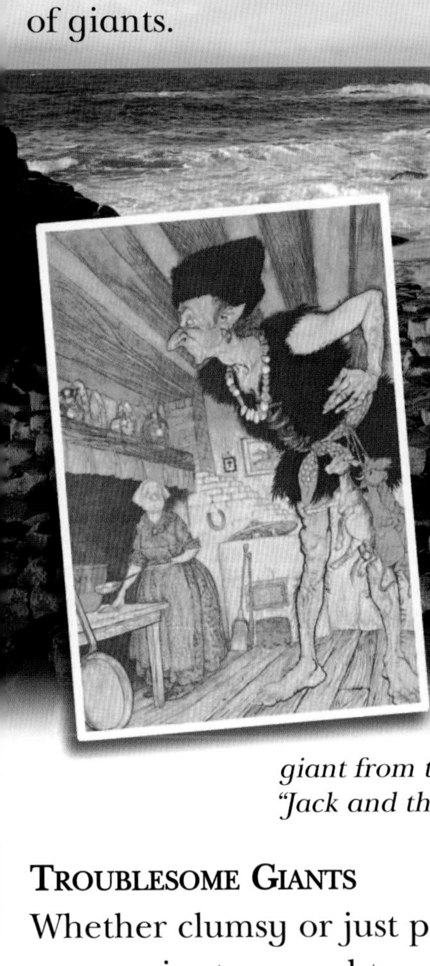

The bad-tempered giant from the fairy tale "Jack and the Beanstalk"

Troublesome Giants

Whether clumsy or just plain mean, giants caused trouble. They stole cattle and drank rivers dry. Their fighting made the ground shake. To fearful humans, they were the forces of mayhem.

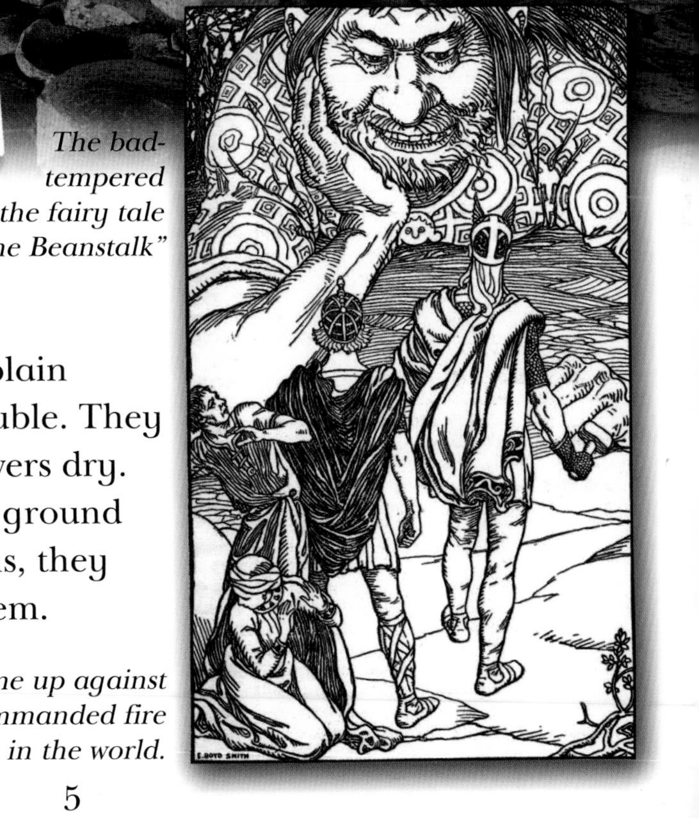

The god Thor often came up against giants. Some Norse giants commanded fire and ice — important elements in the world.

THOR IN THE LAND OF THE GIANTS

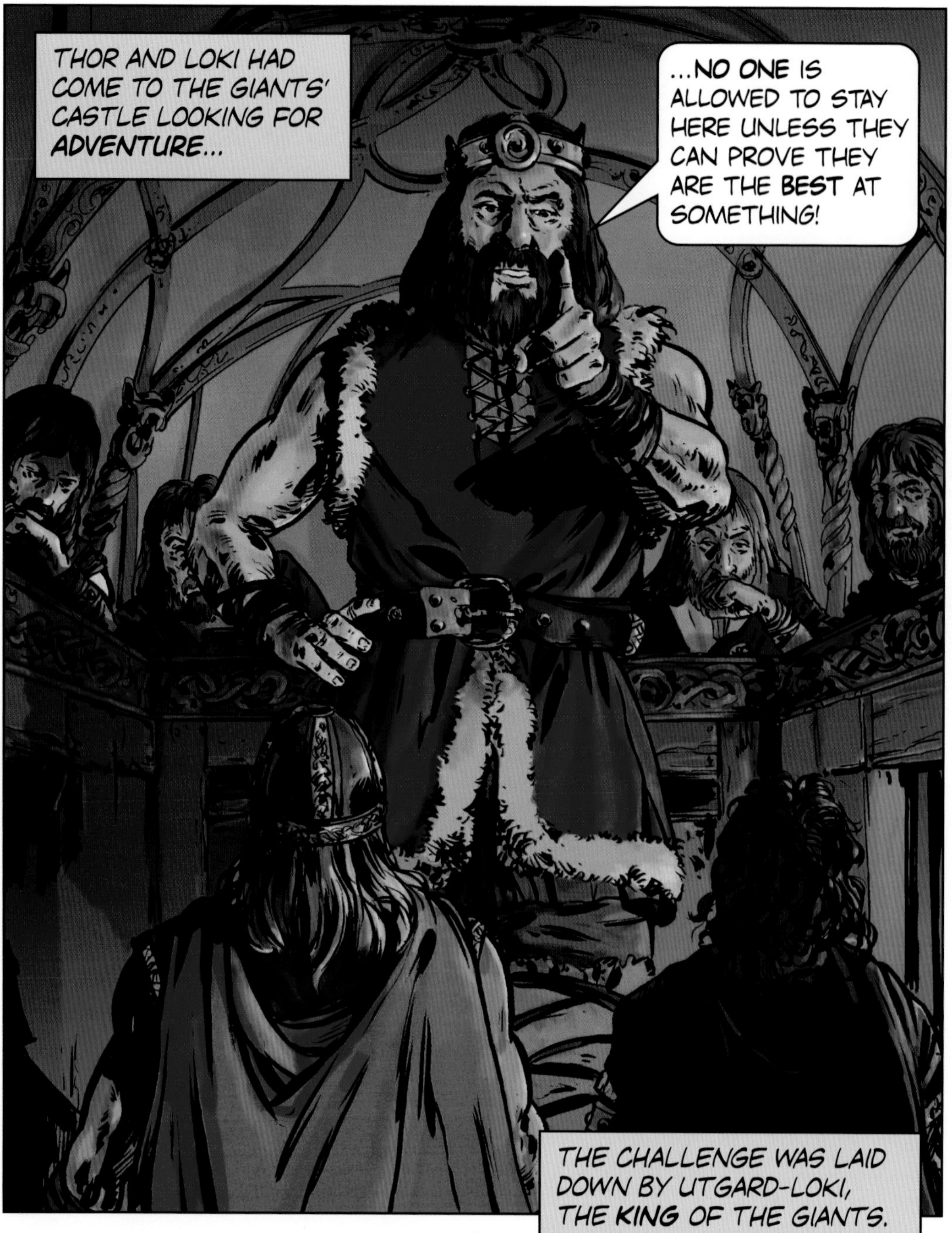
THOR AND LOKI HAD COME TO THE GIANTS' CASTLE LOOKING FOR ADVENTURE...
...NO ONE IS ALLOWED TO STAY HERE UNLESS THEY CAN PROVE THEY ARE THE BEST AT SOMETHING!
THE CHALLENGE WAS LAID DOWN BY UTGARD-LOKI, THE KING OF THE GIANTS.

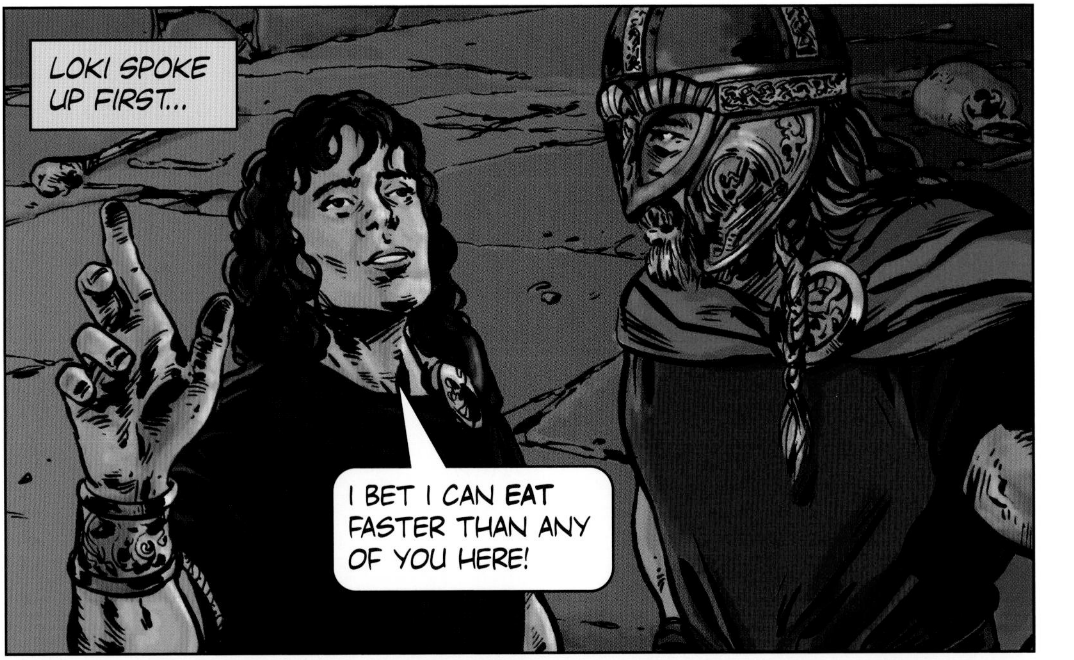
LOKI SPOKE UP FIRST...
I BET I CAN EAT FASTER THAN ANY OF YOU HERE!

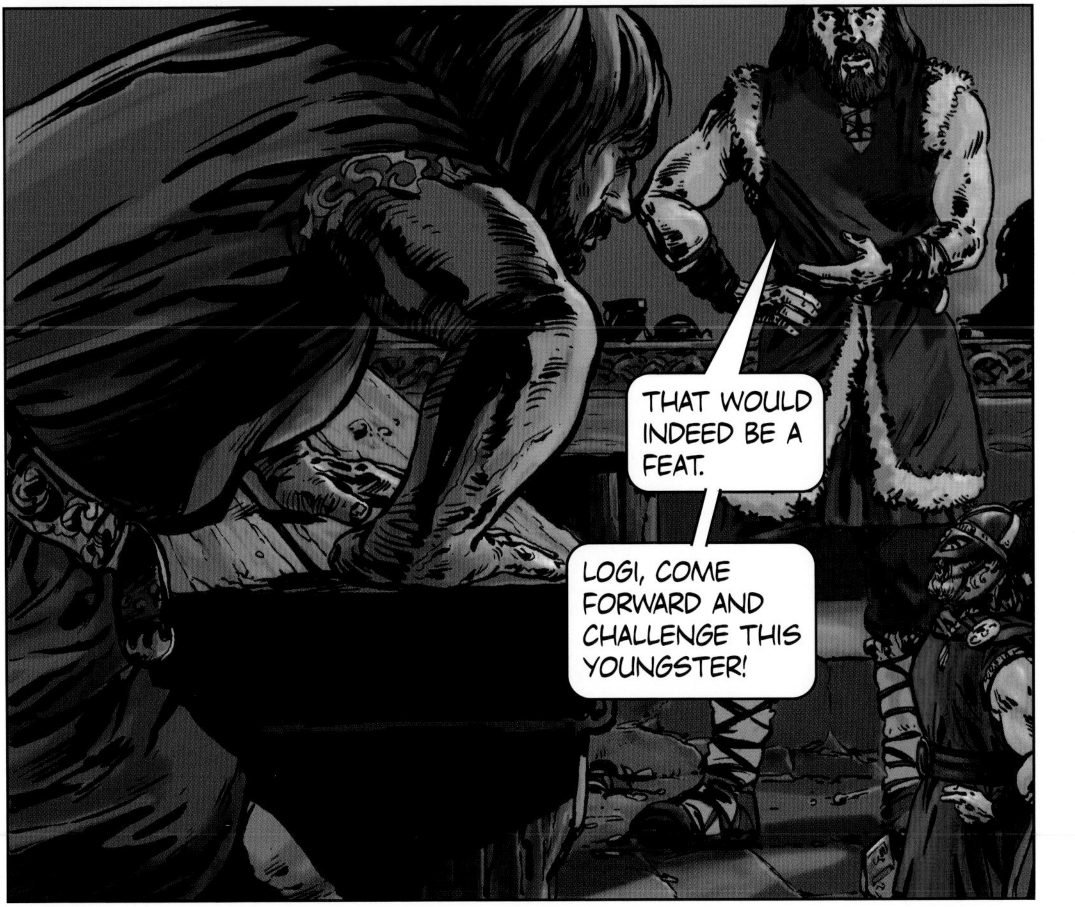
THAT WOULD INDEED BE A FEAT.
LOGI, COME FORWARD AND CHALLENGE THIS YOUNGSTER!

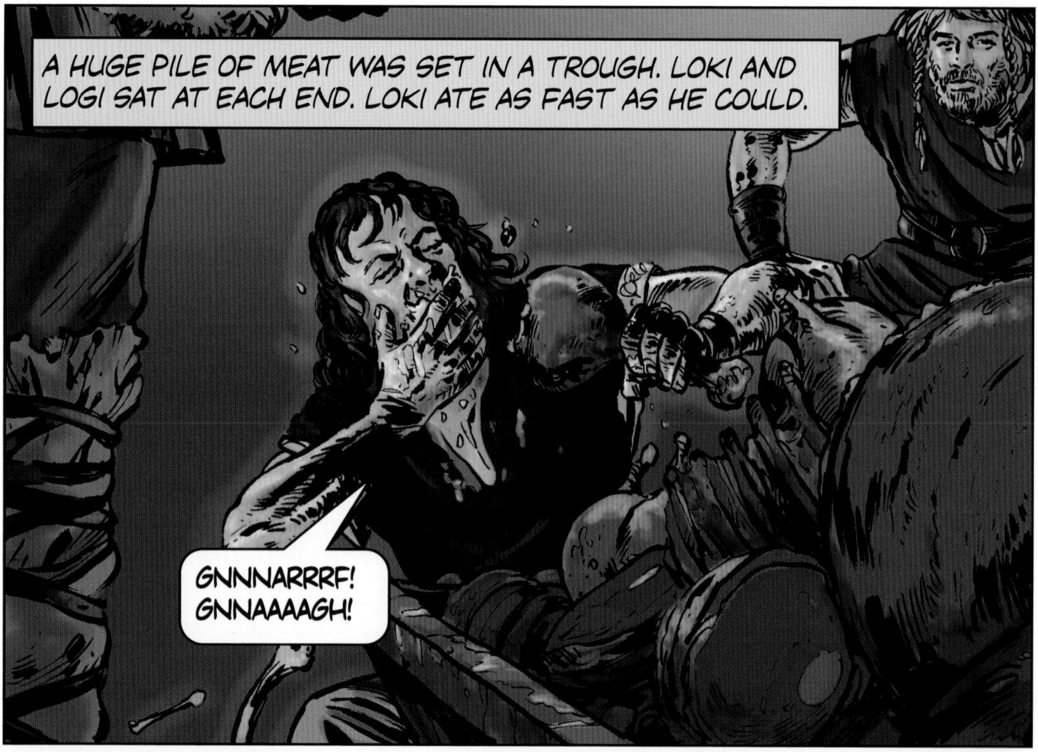
A HUGE PILE OF MEAT WAS SET IN A TROUGH. LOKI AND LOGI SAT AT EACH END. LOKI ATE AS FAST AS HE COULD.
GNNNARRRF! GNNAAAAGH!

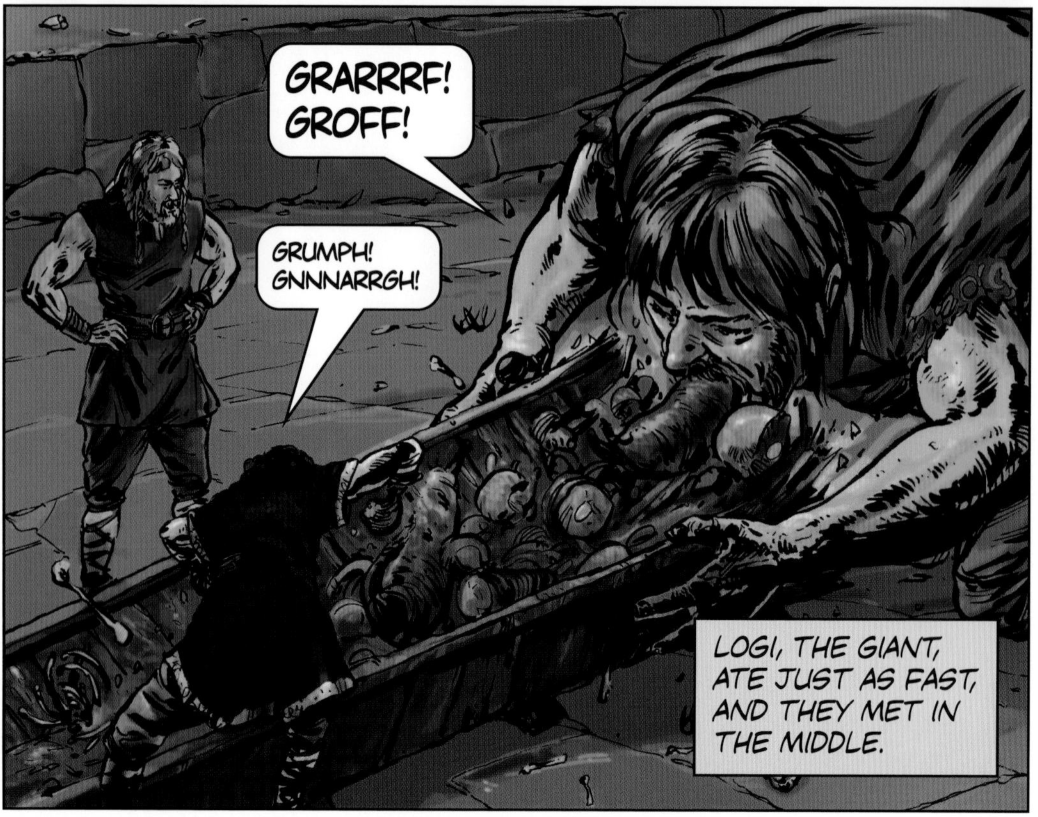
GRARRRF! GROFF!
GRUMPH! GNNNARRGH!
LOGI, THE GIANT, ATE JUST AS FAST, AND THEY MET IN THE MIDDLE.

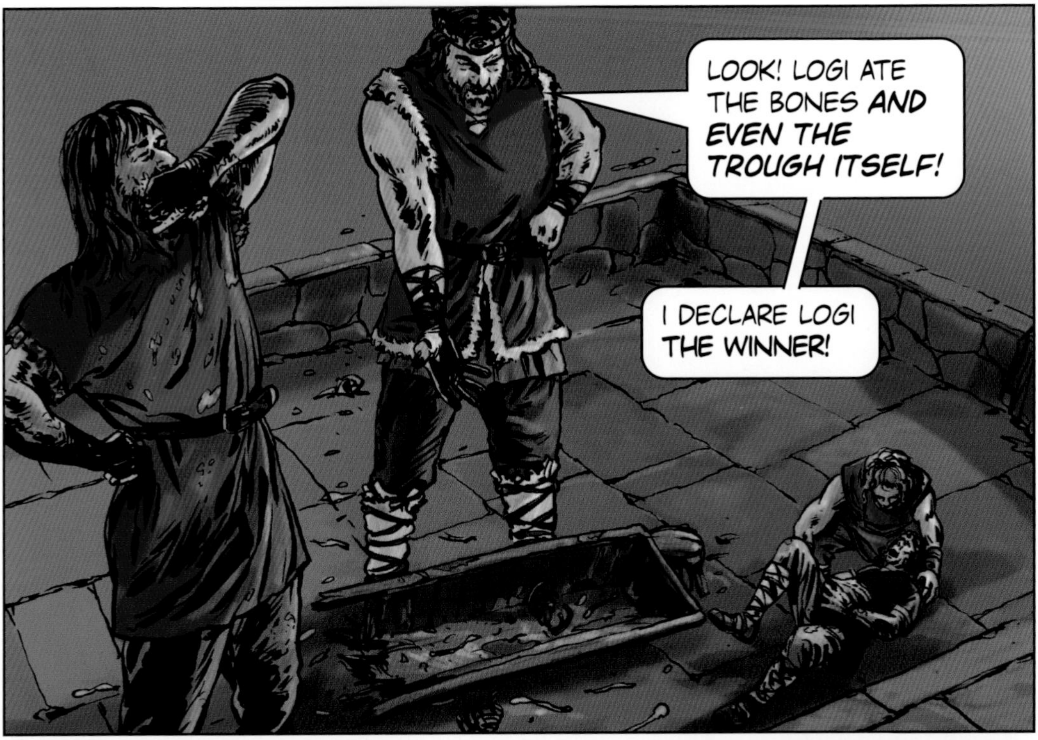
LOOK! LOGI ATE THE BONES AND EVEN THE TROUGH ITSELF!
I DECLARE LOGI THE WINNER!

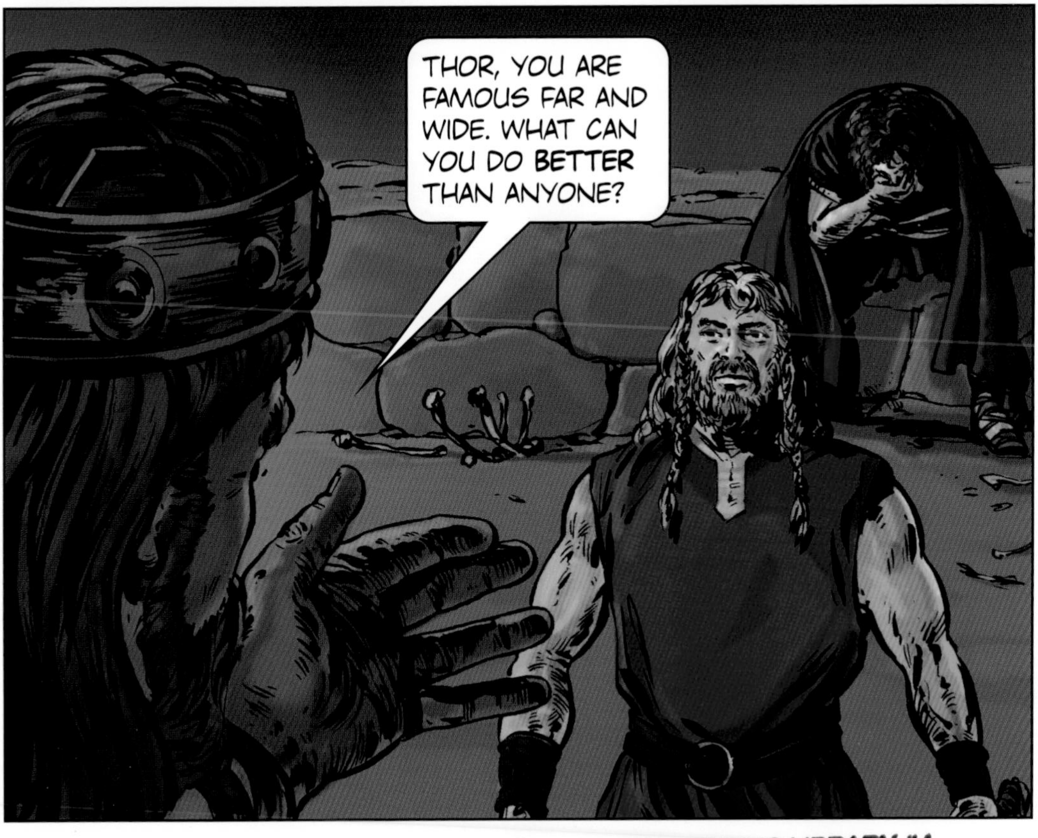
THOR, YOU ARE FAMOUS FAR AND WIDE. WHAT CAN YOU DO BETTER THAN ANYONE?

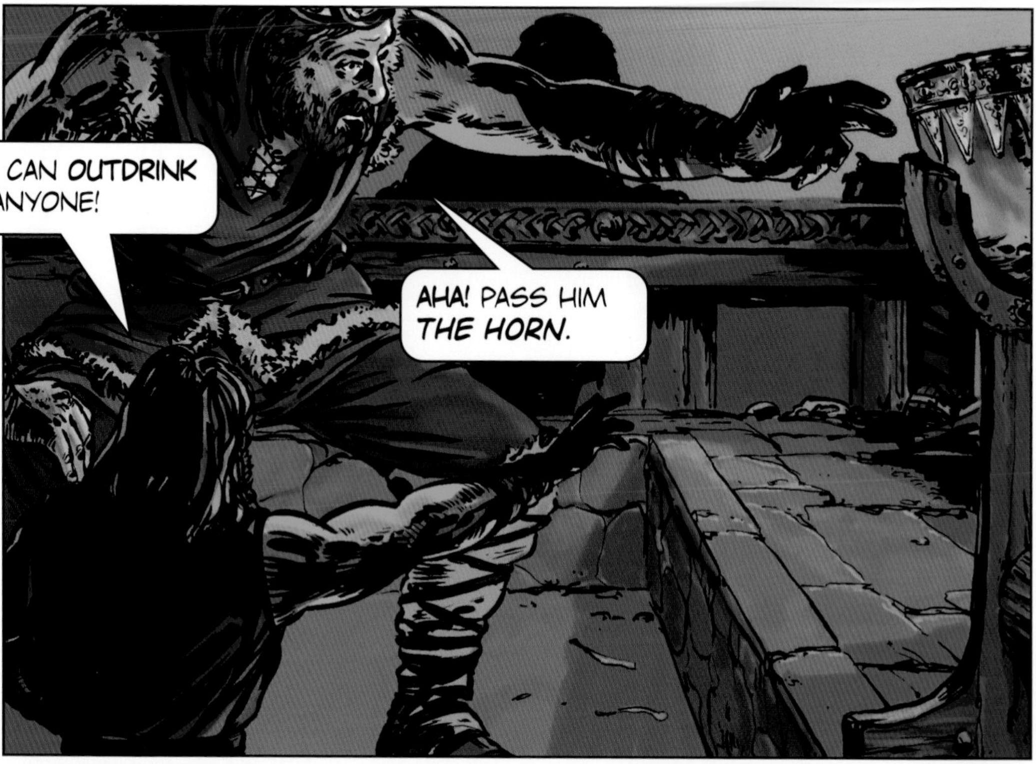
I CAN OUTDRINK ANYONE!
AHA! PASS HIM THE HORN.

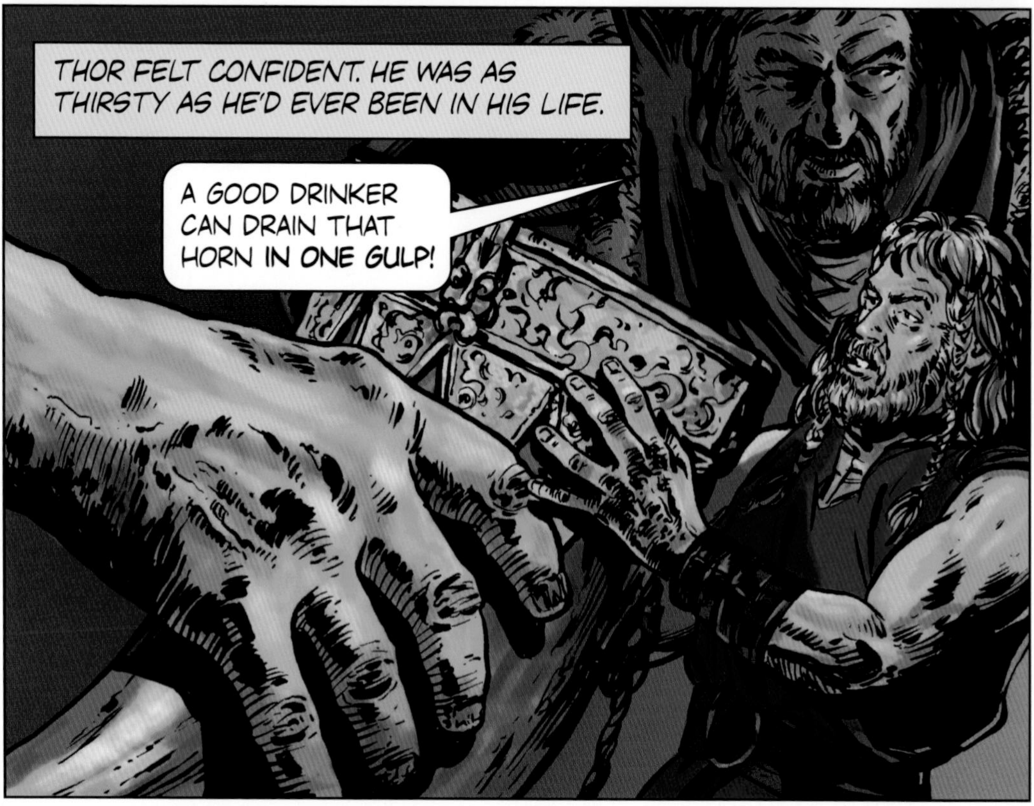
THOR FELT CONFIDENT. HE WAS AS THIRSTY AS HE'D EVER BEEN IN HIS LIFE.
A GOOD DRINKER CAN DRAIN THAT HORN IN ONE GULP!

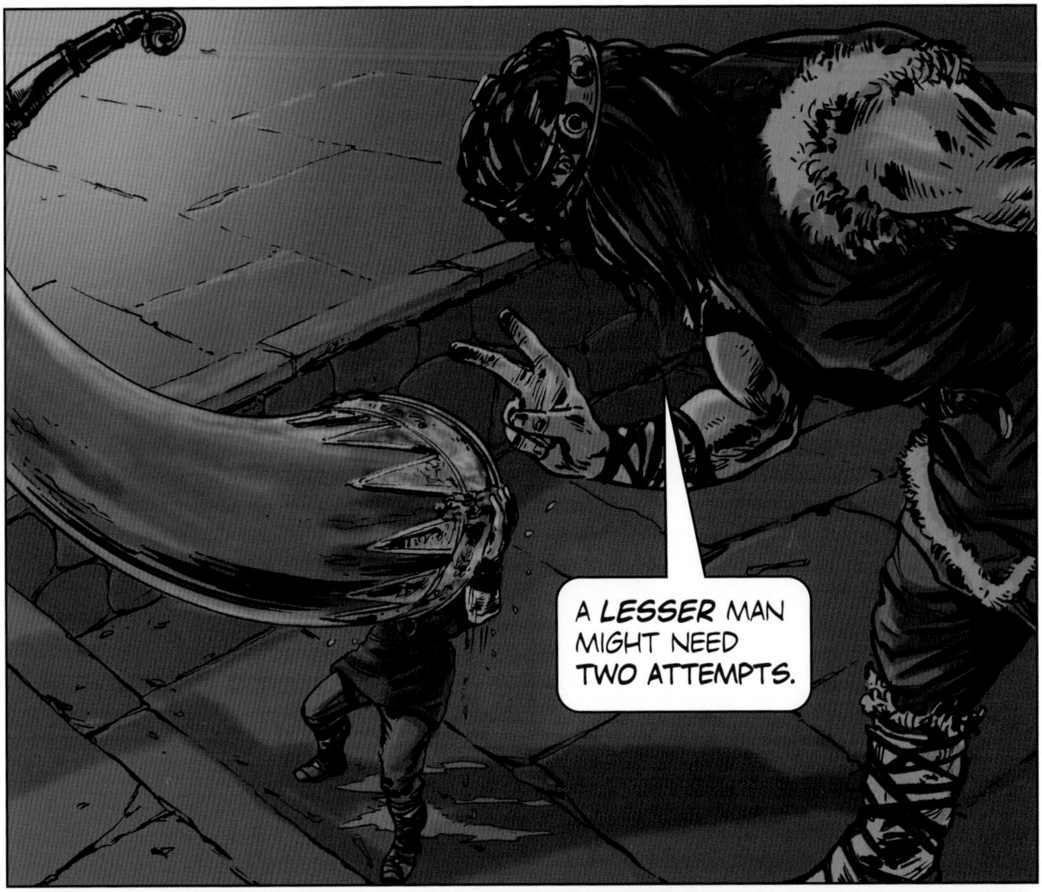
A LESSER MAN MIGHT NEED TWO ATTEMPTS.

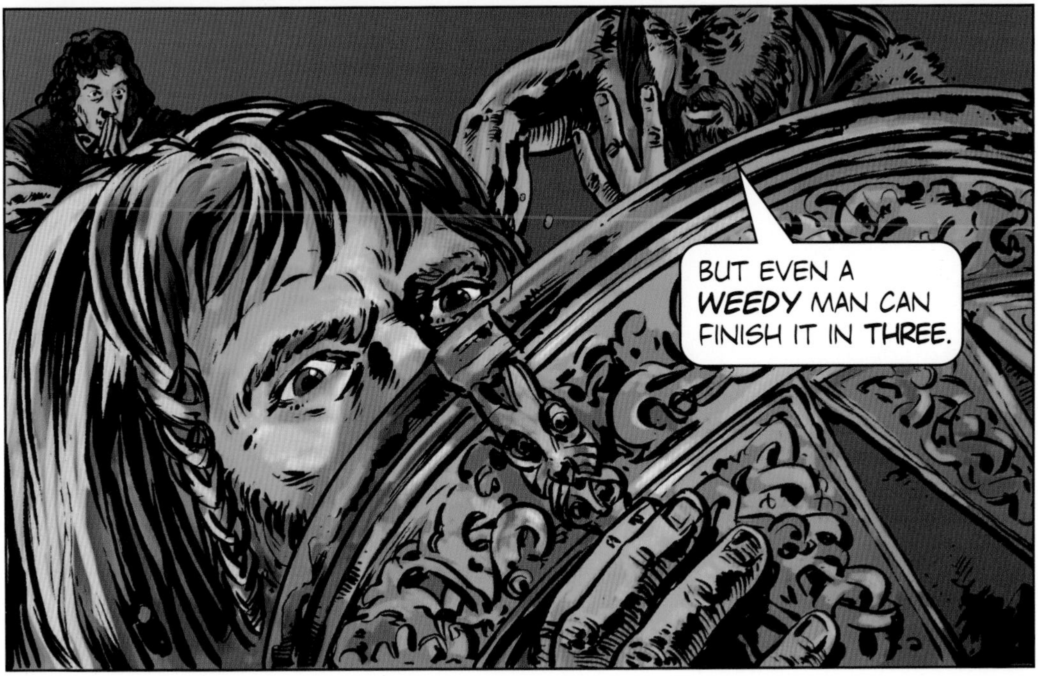
BUT EVEN A WEEDY MAN CAN FINISH IT IN THREE.

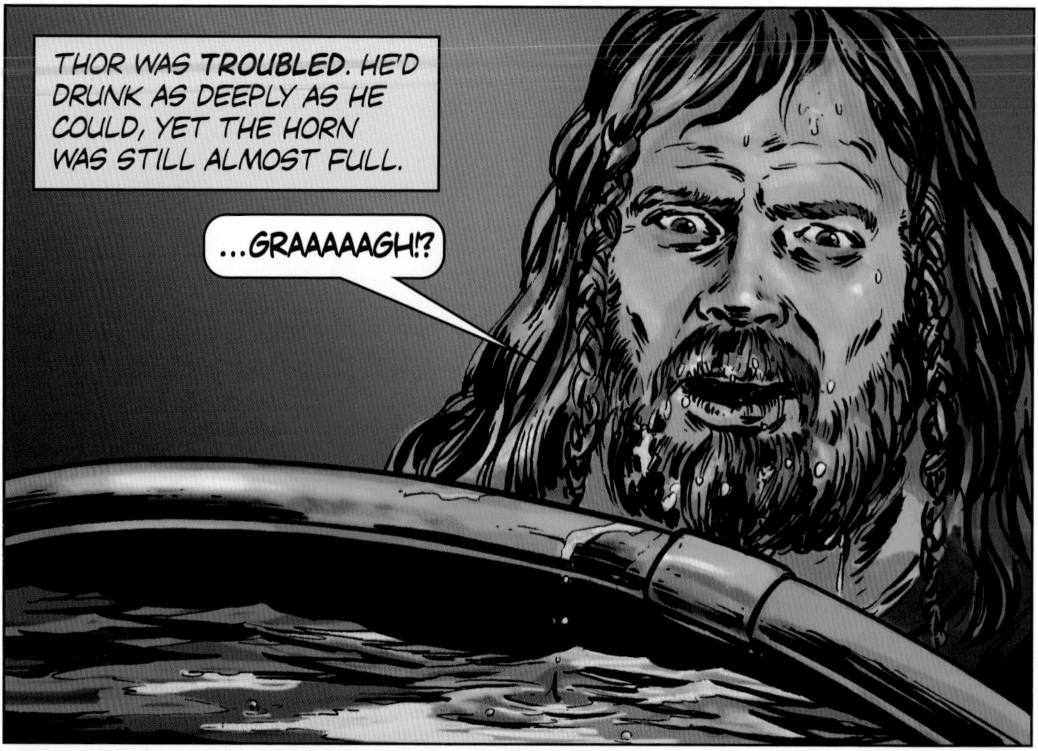
THOR WAS TROUBLED. HE'D DRUNK AS DEEPLY AS HE COULD, YET THE HORN WAS STILL ALMOST FULL.
...GRAAAAAGH!?

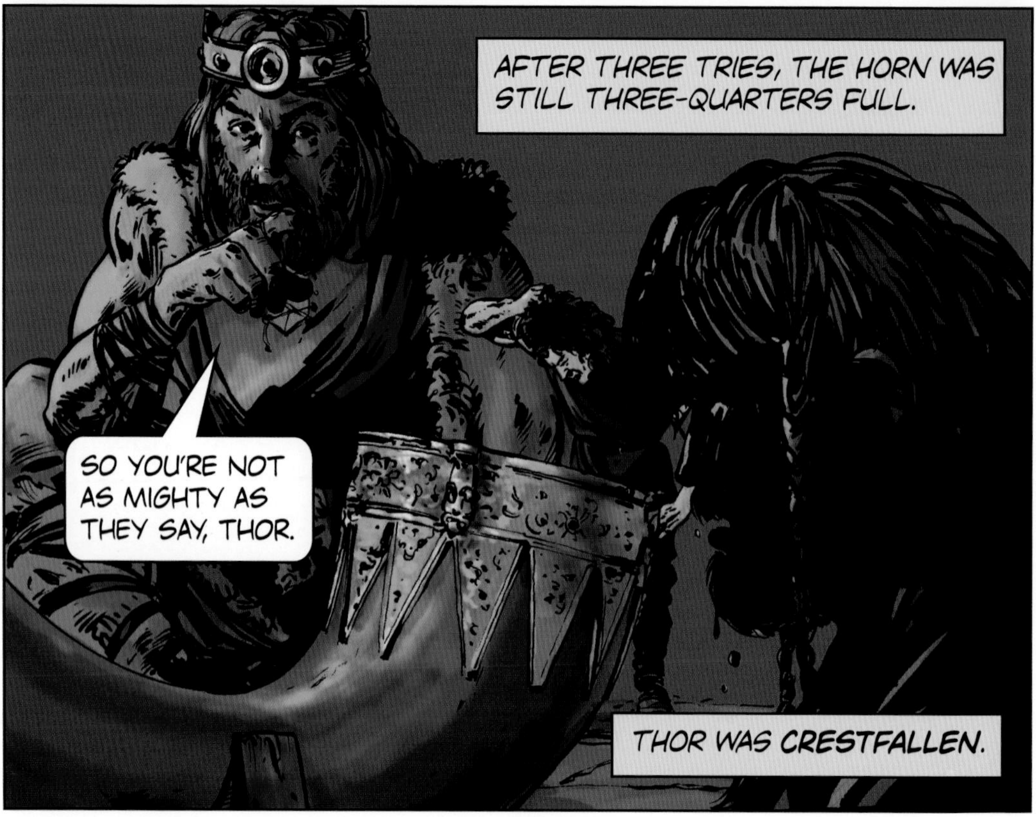
AFTER THREE TRIES, THE HORN WAS STILL THREE-QUARTERS FULL.
SO YOU'RE NOT AS MIGHTY AS THEY SAY, THOR.
THOR WAS CRESTFALLEN.

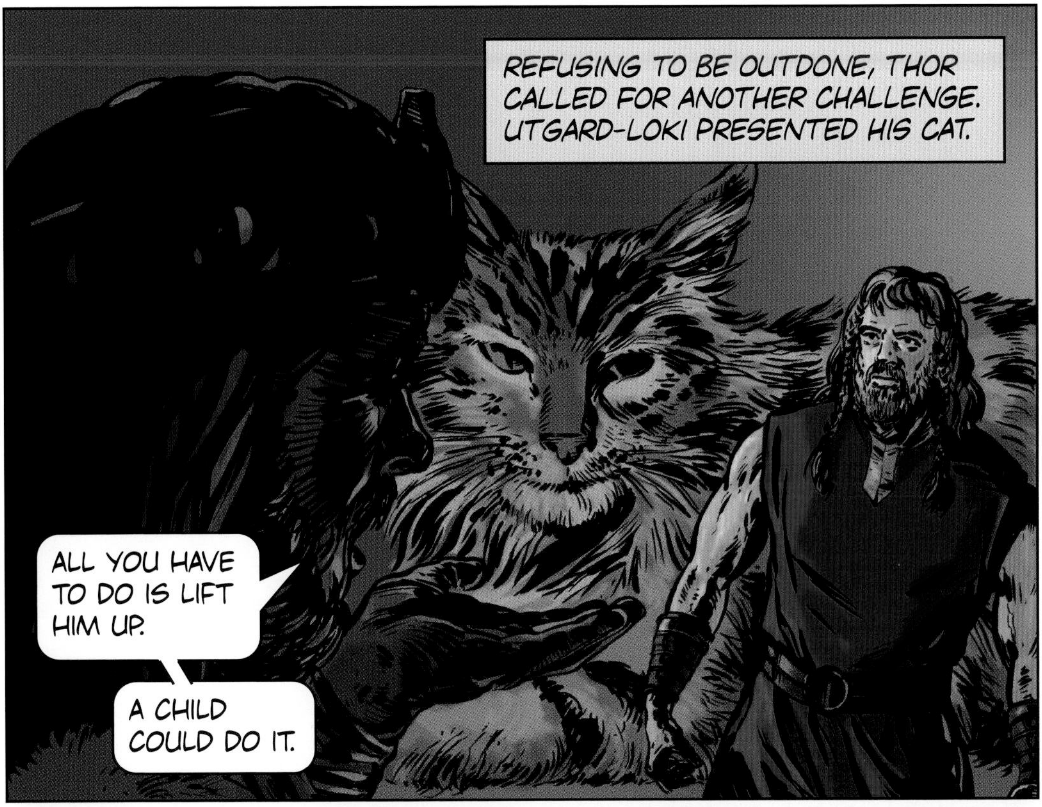
REFUSING TO BE OUTDONE, THOR CALLED FOR ANOTHER CHALLENGE. UTGARD-LOKI PRESENTED HIS CAT.
ALL YOU HAVE TO DO IS LIFT HIM UP.
A CHILD COULD DO IT.

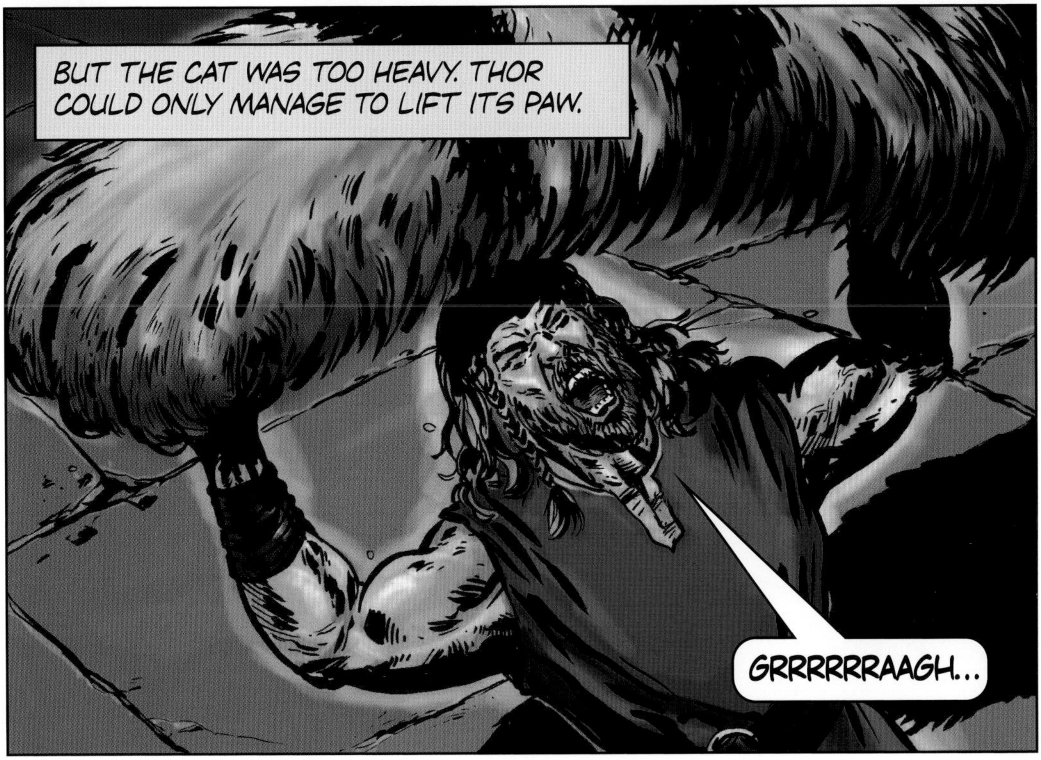
BUT THE CAT WAS TOO HEAVY. THOR COULD ONLY MANAGE TO LIFT ITS PAW.
GRRRRRRAAGH...

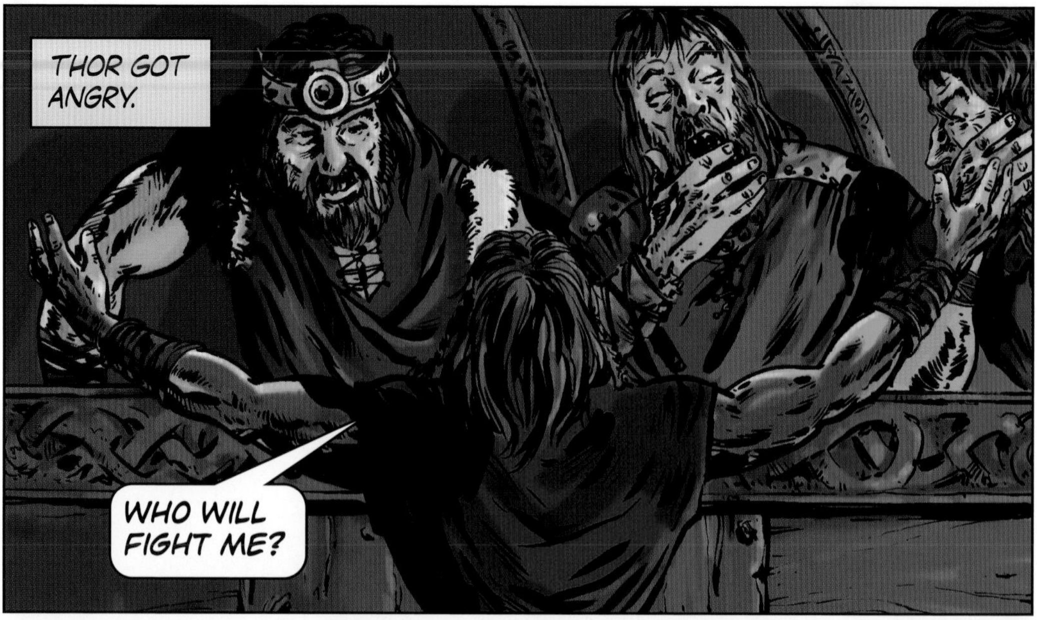
THOR GOT ANGRY.
WHO WILL FIGHT ME?

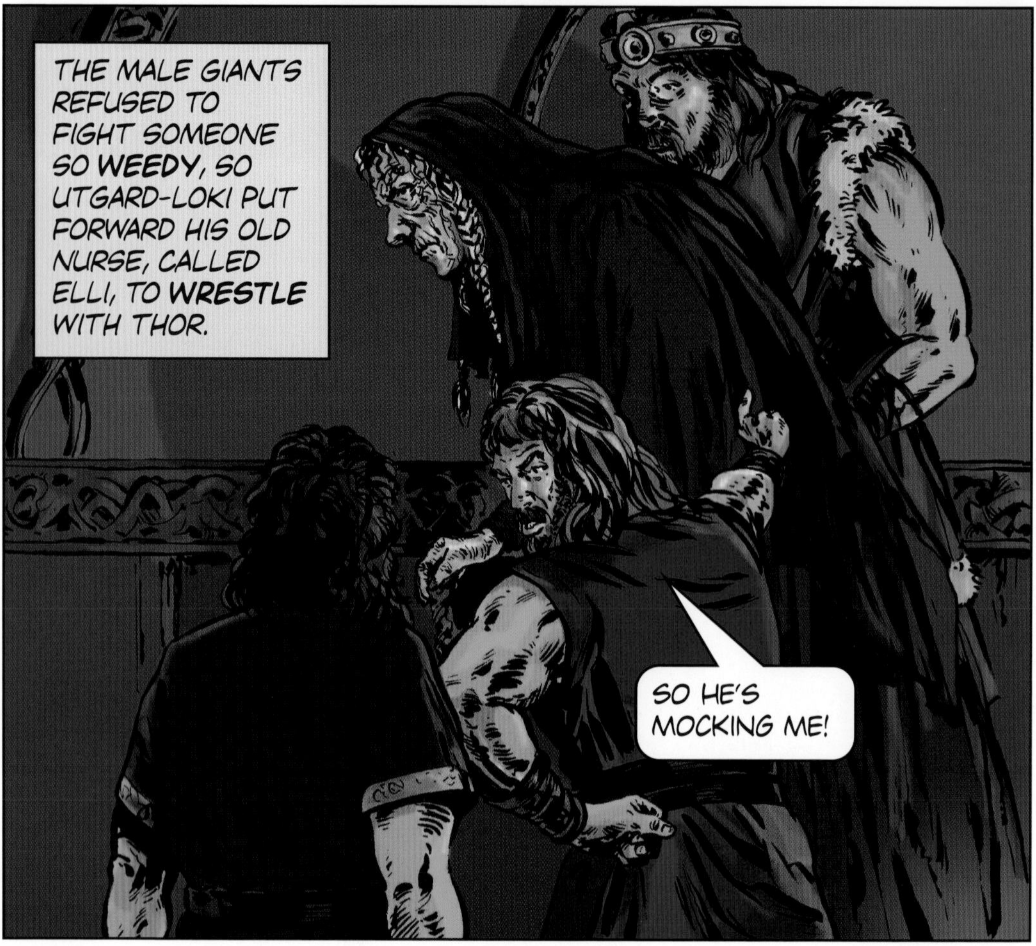
THE MALE GIANTS REFUSED TO FIGHT SOMEONE SO WEEDY, SO UTGARD-LOKI PUT FORWARD HIS OLD NURSE, CALLED ELLI, TO WRESTLE WITH THOR.
SO HE'S MOCKING ME!

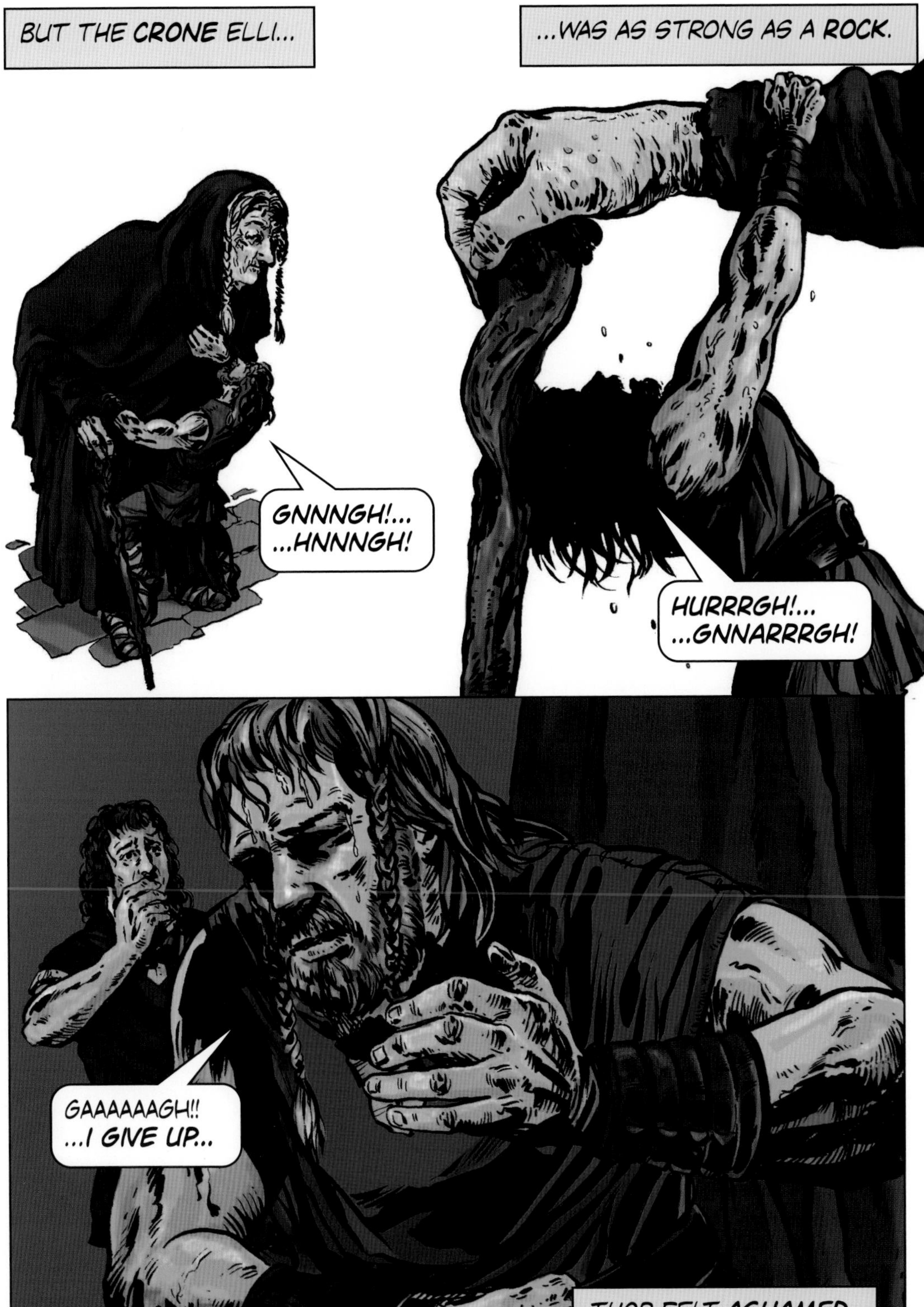
BUT THE CRONE ELLI...
...WAS AS STRONG AS A ROCK.
GNNNGH!... ...HNNNGH!
HURRRGH!... ...GNNARRRGH!
GAAAAAAGH!! ...I GIVE UP...
THOR FELT ASHAMED.

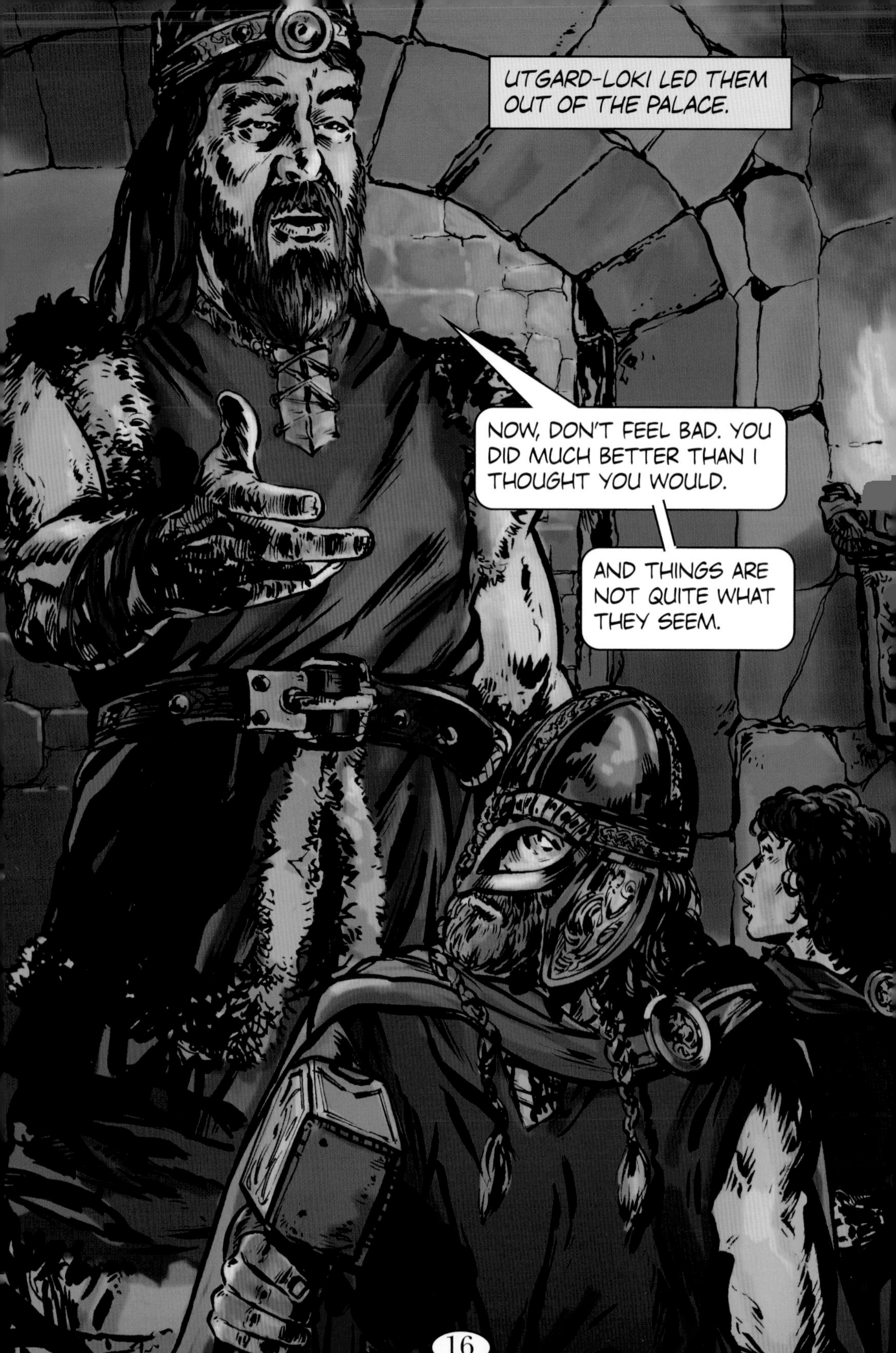
UTGARD-LOKI LED THEM OUT OF THE PALACE.
NOW, DON'T FEEL BAD. YOU DID MUCH BETTER THAN I THOUGHT YOU WOULD.
AND THINGS ARE NOT QUITE WHAT THEY SEEM.

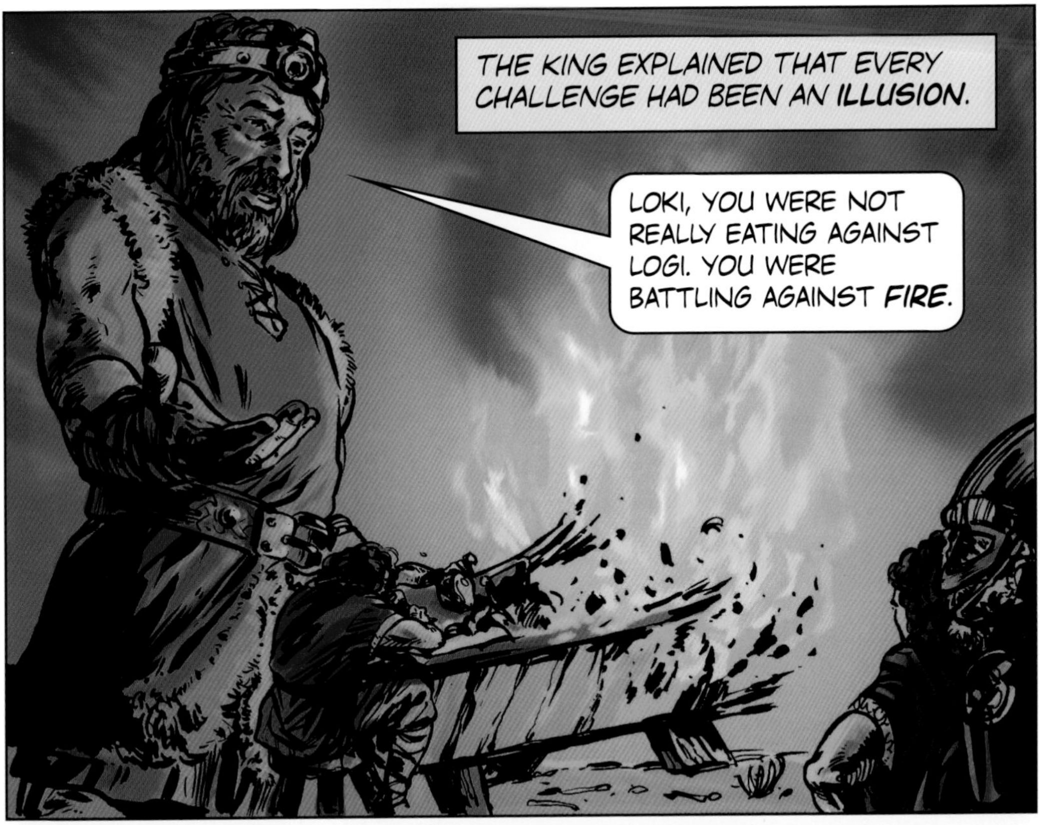
THE KING EXPLAINED THAT EVERY CHALLENGE HAD BEEN AN **ILLUSION**.
LOKI, YOU WERE NOT REALLY EATING AGAINST LOGI. YOU WERE BATTLING AGAINST ***FIRE***.

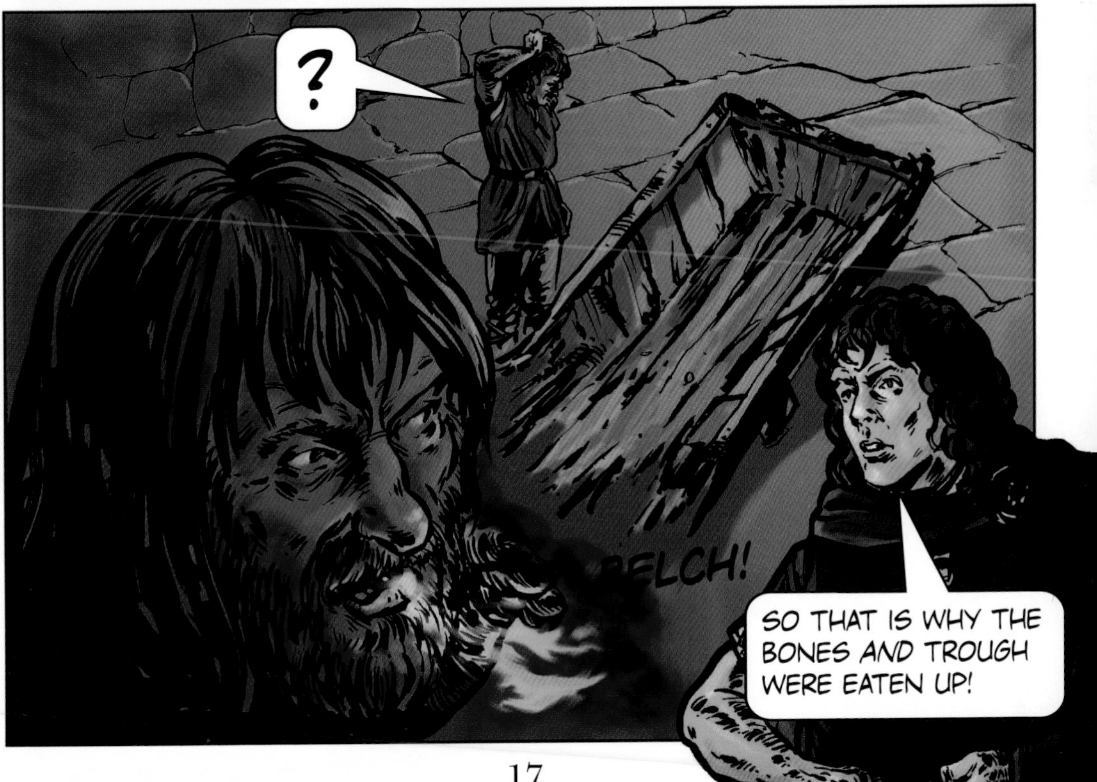
?
SO THAT IS WHY THE BONES AND TROUGH WERE EATEN UP!

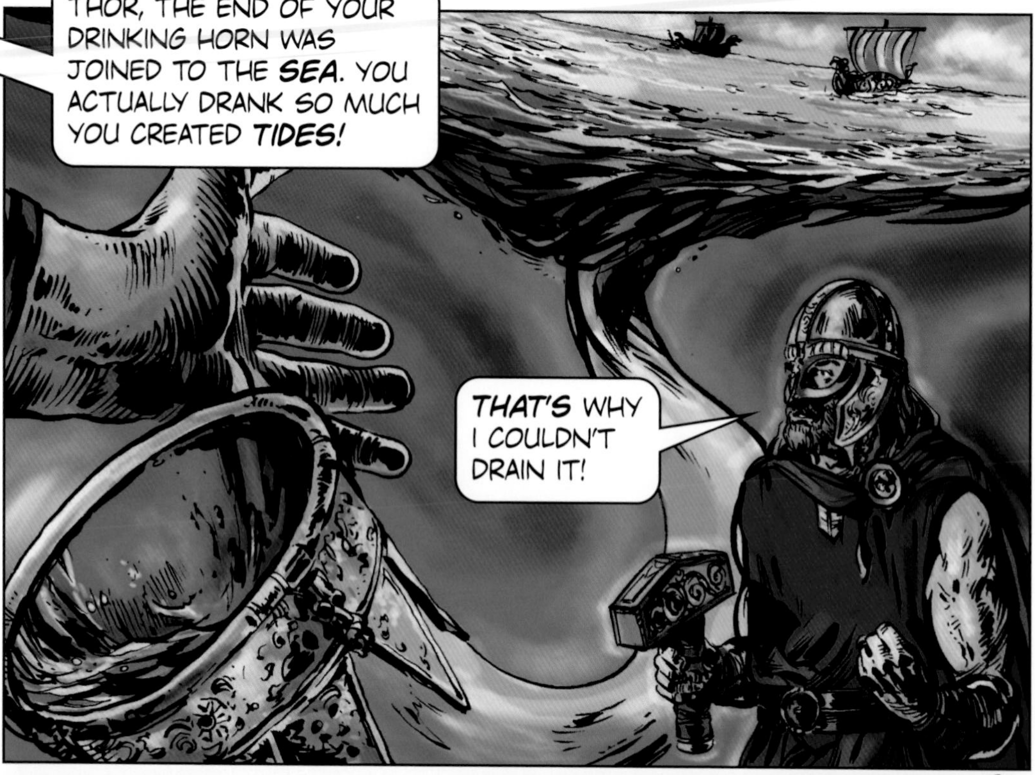
THOR, THE END OF YOUR DRINKING HORN WAS JOINED TO THE **SEA**. YOU ACTUALLY DRANK SO MUCH YOU CREATED **TIDES!**
THAT'S WHY I COULDN'T DRAIN IT!

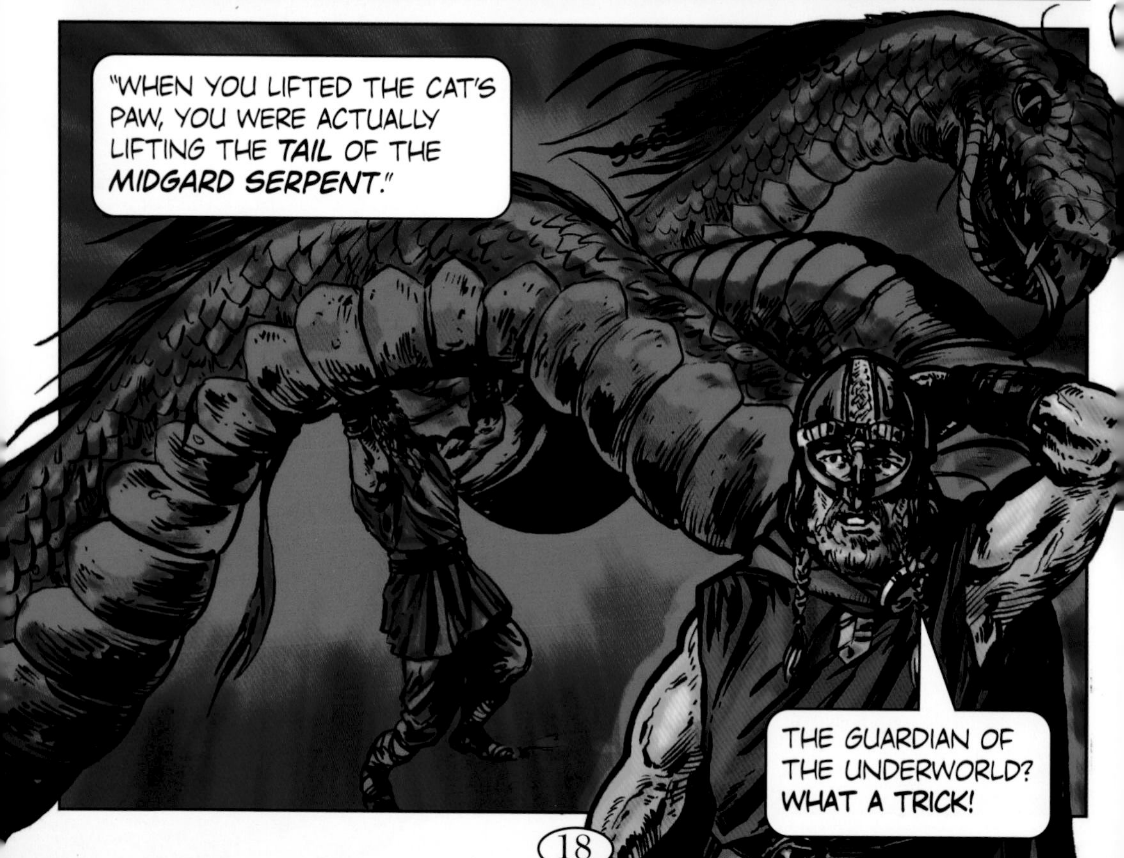
"WHEN YOU LIFTED THE CAT'S PAW, YOU WERE ACTUALLY LIFTING THE **TAIL** OF THE **MIDGARD SERPENT**."
THE GUARDIAN OF THE UNDERWORLD? **WHAT A TRICK!**

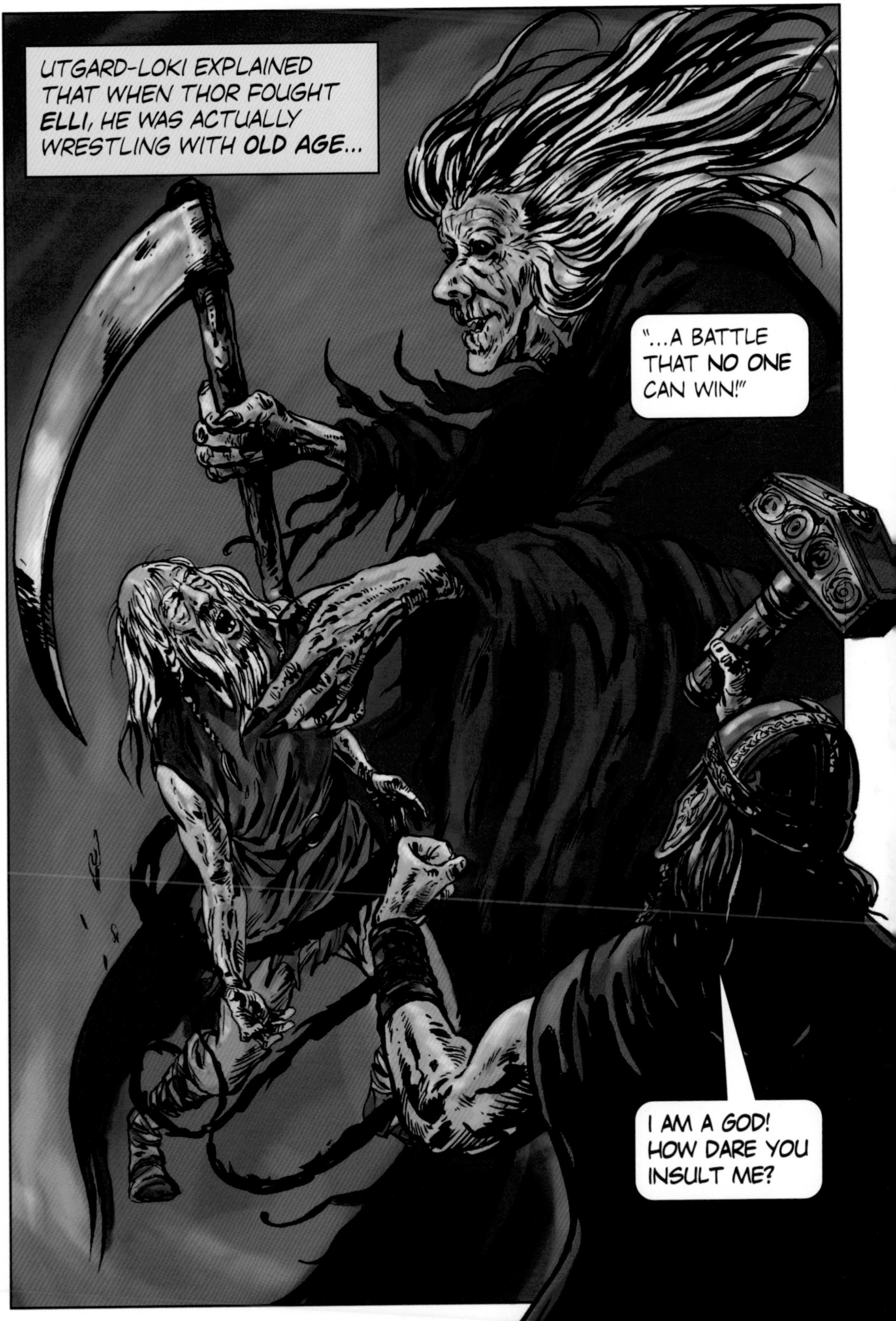
UTGARD-LOKI EXPLAINED THAT WHEN THOR FOUGHT **ELLI**, HE WAS ACTUALLY WRESTLING WITH **OLD AGE**...
"...A BATTLE THAT **NO ONE** CAN WIN!"
I AM A GOD! HOW DARE YOU INSULT ME?

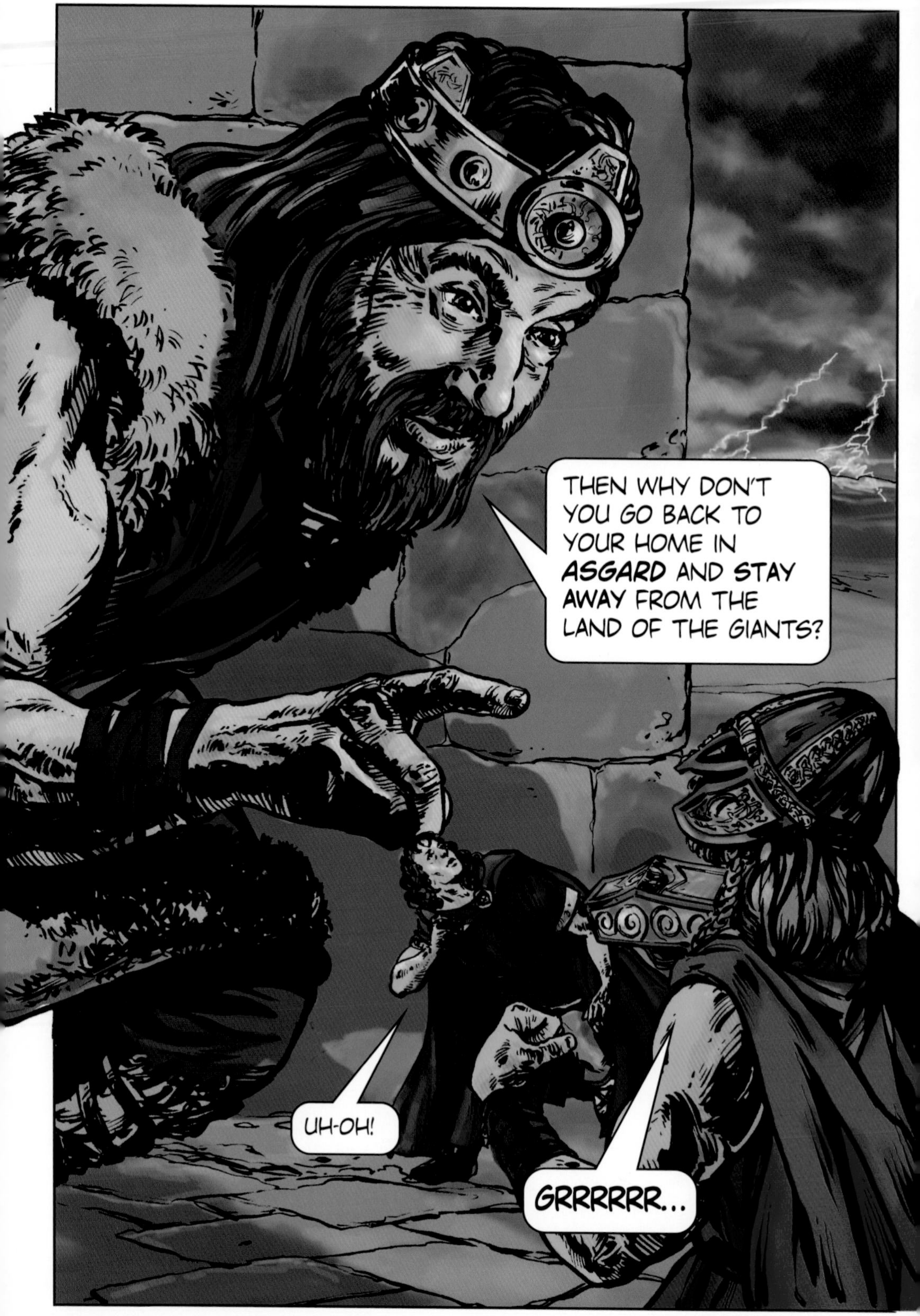
THEN WHY DON'T YOU GO BACK TO YOUR HOME IN **ASGARD** AND **STAY AWAY** FROM THE LAND OF THE GIANTS?
UH-OH!
GRRRRRR...

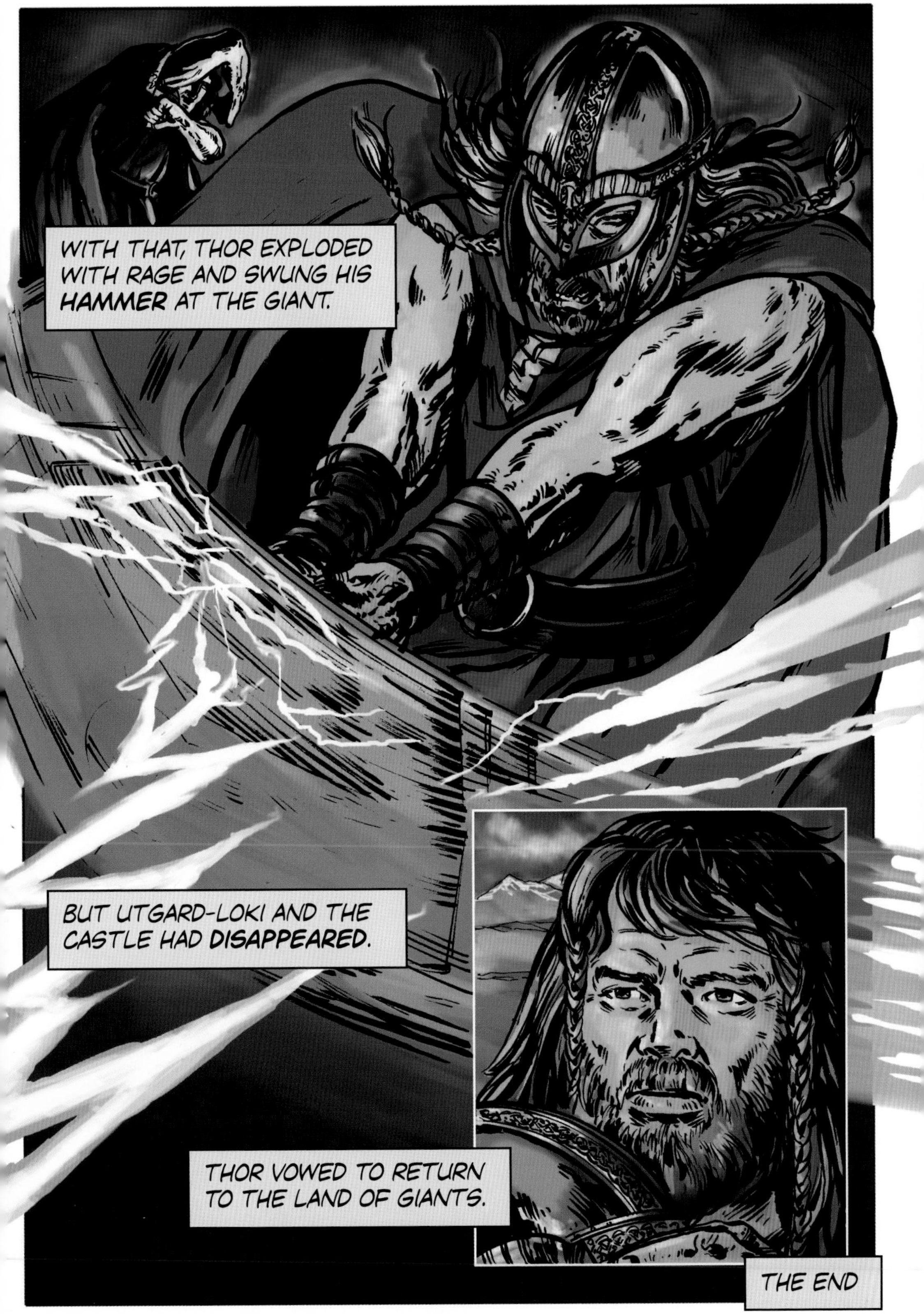
WITH THAT, THOR EXPLODED WITH RAGE AND SWUNG HIS HAMMER AT THE GIANT.
BUT UTGARD-LOKI AND THE CASTLE HAD DISAPPEARED.
THOR VOWED TO RETURN TO THE LAND OF GIANTS.
THE END

Other Gigantic Tales

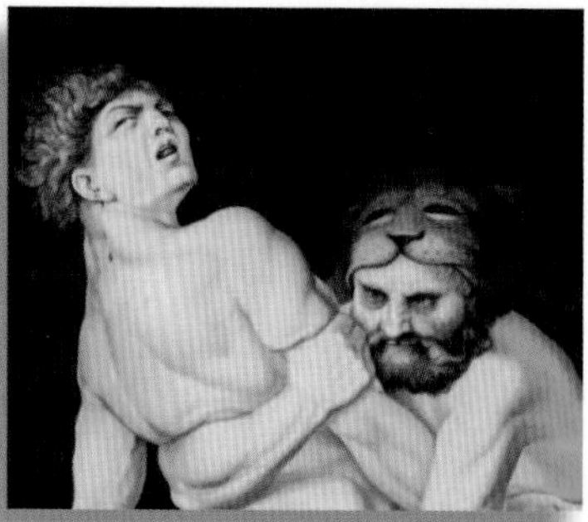
Herakles crushes Antaeus.

Thor did return to the land of the giants for more adventures. Listed below are some other well-known stories featuring larger-than-life characters.

Herakles and Antaeus
The Greek hero Herakles wrestles with a murderous Libyan giant called Antaeus and finds his weakness.

Haymo and the Dragon
The good Austrian giant Haymo saves a village from the terrors of a dragon.

The Myth of Cabracan
Cabracan, a Mayan giant, is the size of a mountain. When he is angry, he causes earthquakes. A pair of human hero twins decide to take him on.

Finn McCool
Celtic giant Finn McCool argues hotly with a rival giant. In a fury, he scoops up a huge lump of land and throws it into the ocean. The place where it lands becomes an island.

Kumbhakarna
After being asleep for six months, the huge Indian giant Kumbhakarna wakes up feeling terribly hungry. He grabs trees, bushes, rocks, and humans that are in the way.

The awakening of Kumbhakarna

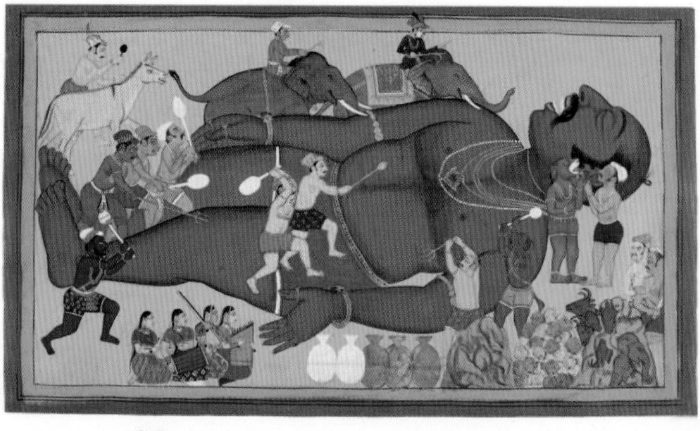

GLOSSARY

ashamed Feeling embarrassed and sometimes guilty because of your behavior or performance.

clumsy Lacking physical coordination and skill in movement.

crestfallen Feeling disheartened and discouraged.

crone An ugly, withered old woman.

demon An evil spirit.

handiwork Something made or done by a particular person or creature.

illusion An unreal idea or image that creates a false impression.

landmark A prominent feature of the landscape that identifies a particular place.

legendary Relating to a legend, which is a story passed down through history.

mayhem A state of violent disorder and confusion.

mocking Making fun of and insulting.

trough A long, narrow open container holding water or food for animals.

weedy Having a thin, bony, and weak build.

INDEX